FIONA FINDS HER PURPOSE:

The Story of a Black Lab, Two African Wild Dog Pups and Their Brief Encounter

Published by Mission Point Press
2554 Chandler Rd.
Traverse City, MI 49696
(231) 421-9513
www.MissionPointPress.com

Design by Sarah Meiers
Illustrations by: Dereck Boven
African wild dog photographs courtesy of: @windows2thewild

ISBN 978-1-961302-12-9 (hardcover)
ISBN 978-1-961302-26-6 (softcover)
Library of Congress Control Number 2023914699

Printed in the United States of America

FIONA FINDS HER PURPOSE:

The Story of
a Black Lab,
Two African
Wild Dog Pups,
and Their
Brief Encounter

Karen Rieser

MISSION POINT PRESS

Dedication

**Written in memory of Fiona Laird,
a dearly loved rescued black lab.**

Contents

Preface

◆ ◆ ◆

BLACK ELK, a mid-eighteenth-century medicine man of the Oglala Lakota, described our essence as being "…related to all things; the Earth and the stars, everything." For many the wisdom of these words is all encompassing. It relays the message that survival is connected to the health and wellness of the Earth, its flora, and its fauna. Today (2023) our planet is experiencing global warming in addition to plant and animal extinction. Fortunately, many people and organizations are attending to this concern, one such organization is the zoological park.

Many modern zoos are in touch with Black Elk's wisdom. They are no longer just a place to take a Sunday stroll and view caged animals. Zoos currently are investing time and money into scientific research aimed at preserving and maintaining a healthy physical, emotional, and ecologically appropriate environment for all life to share.

In *Fiona Finds Her Purpose* you will read about the Association of Zoos and Aquariums or AZA. The AZA is a non-profit organization that promotes the advancement of conservation, education, science, and recreation in zoos and aquariums. The standards required to be accredited by the AZA are the highest for animal care and welfare. An AZA accredited facility employs highly trained professionals and is considered to have outstanding conservation programs running alongside public recreation.

Under the umbrella of the AZA there are a variety of projects to consider, one of which is creating, running, and supporting a Species Survival Plan. You will read about such a plan in 'Fiona Finds Her Purpose'. Animal conservationists classify animals as extinct, extinct in the wild, critically endangered, endangered, vulnerable, near threatened and least concern. Species Survival Plans are drawn up by an animal specialist for extinct in the wild, critically endangered and endangered animals; in this case a specialist for the African wild dog. The goal of the plan is to ensure a healthy, genetically diverse, and demographically varied animal population.

A specialist works with all AZA facilities when developing and implementing the plan.

'The Humane Society of America' was founded in 1877 to promote humane treatment of children and animals. In 1954 its name changed to 'The Humane Society of the United States' (HSUS). The HSUS works on legislation to prevent animal cruelty, investigates questionable situations, provides public education, and has a large network providing animal adoption services.

With this knowledge please enjoy *Fiona Finds Her Purpose*.

CHAPTER ONE

A Long Way from Africa

* * *

ALWAYS THE FIRST TO BOARD THE TRAM at the Foxmoore Area Zoo's Transport Center, Alice greeted George with the briefest of hellos. She felt quite frazzled, having just battled the early morning traffic into Foxmoore. Those who didn't know better would never have guessed that the eastern edge of this bustling metropolis sheltered a delightful oasis containing woods, streams, and exotic animals from all over the world.

Letting out a nervous sigh at odds with the peaceful early morning, the young zookeeper slid onto the smooth wooden bench. The air smelled of sweet earthy dew, and leafy shadows floated here and there as a moist breeze wafted through the car.

"Those dogs be waitin' for you, Alice. Gonna be a good day to sleep in the sun."

"I hope so, George. I'm a bit nervous. Today will be the first time I speak to our guests about my dogs."

"It'll be all right," the driver nodded. "Don't you worry."

Alice leaned back as the tram began its climb up the hilly, gravel-covered road leading to the African exhibit, her home away from home. Closing her eyes, she listened to the birds calling to the humming of the tram's engine and the leaves fluttering in the breeze. Most of the zoo's grounds had been left in nature's care, with the exception of the road they were traveling and the all-but-invisible black chain link fence surrounding the property.

The tram wound its way left, passing through a swamp. Storms had felled trees, causing them to crisscross several small ponds, showing off Mother Nature's skill at creating fabulous wooden sculptures. By noon, these sculptures would be covered with sunbathing turtles, while the tree frogs now singing loud and clear would be silent. The very air smelled green as they crossed the stream meandering through the park.

After a short five-minute ride, Alice sat up. They had arrived.

She took a deep breath as the tram's speaker made the first of many announcements of the day. "Africa — A Wildlife Experience. Please disembark to your left. Enjoy your day."

The Foxmoore Area Zoo was the pride of North Carolina. It was the only zoo in the United States to have won multiple awards for each of its seven continental exhibits. The African Exhibit was a popular destination, especially in the summer, thanks to its resident herd of giraffes, the largest in the country. Grabbing her cooler and thermos, Alice left the tram and nodded at George before heading for the boardwalk leading to the African wild dog enclosure.

"Take it easy, George."

"Will do," he replied. "And good luck today."

Most people considered zoos to be delightful places to watch exotic animals and perhaps learn a thing or two. This zoo was that but also a great deal more. A member of the Association of Zoos and Aquariums, the Foxmoore Area Zoo offered quality educational, conservation, and research programs while overseeing a great many Species Survival Plans for vulnerable wildlife. Alice had been hired several years earlier to coordinate the Species Survival Plan for African wild dogs.

As far as she was concerned, this was the best job on the entire planet.

She had fallen in love with African wild dogs at the age of ten, when her family had visited Zimbabwe for a year so her parents could take photographs of wildlife for a book promoting African tourism. During that wonderful year, she had accompanied her mom and dad on numerous safaris into the savanna and had been endlessly fascinated by the beautiful dogs in their natural habitat.

When Alice realized the dogs were threatened with extinction, she wanted to help, but this was easier said than done. Local farmers who found their goats half eaten hunted the dogs. These same farmers wanted to grow crops on the savanna. As the dogs' habitat shrank, so did their numbers, until fewer than five thousand remained. All too aware of their vulnerability, Alice had earned her Ph.D. in zoology specializing in the study of African wild dogs. Her early exposure, her desire to protect them, and her studies and training had led her here, to this zoo and this particular pack of dogs.

Charged with creating and managing the African wild dog Species Survival Plan, it was Alice's responsibility to make sure her pack bred well, delivered healthy offspring, and was cared for properly. It was also her job to educate the public regarding the dog's place in the African ecosystem. This required Alice to oversee the efforts of other zoos across the U.S. and Europe in managing their packs of African wild dogs. It was a big job, and she loved every minute of it.

The African exhibit contained multiple enclosures. Foxmoore Area Zoo had taken great pains to design its enclosures to ensure predators and prey never came into contact. Although the predator/prey relationship is very real in nature, it wasn't part of the zoo's mission to display such activity.

Hiking onto the raised wooden boardwalk that gave the visitors a bird's-eye view of a twenty-acre grassland exhibit, Alice glanced at her watch. She'd have to hurry, but she couldn't resist taking a minute to enjoy the sights at each overlook.

At her first stop, she spotted grazing zebra and addra gazelle. She lifted herself up onto her tiptoes but could barely see the golden-feathered heads of the crowned cranes in the tall grasses.

At the next stop, she grabbed a couple of lettuce leaves and fed the doe-eyed giraffes peering over their feeding station. She loved to watch their purple, ribbon-like tongues curl around this succulent treat. Ostrich were nosing about today, too; that meant delicious insects were in the vicinity.

Alice walked on a bit further before entering the wild dog exhibit through the keeper's door that led to her office, its entrance camouflaged with vines growing from the trees above.

From her office, she entered the wild dog holding area. The dogs were in their pens behind the glass windows of the keeper's walkway. She went directly to the keeper's observation area to take the day's first look at the exhibit.

It had taken Alice a year and a half to create the perfect ecosystem. Her dogs might be a long way from Africa, but it was her job to recreate their natural environment to the best of her ability.

For ideas, she had looked to the animals of her youth. She knew the animals needed opportunities to be social, to forage, and to practice being predators, an activity that was often unintentionally comical. Exploring, being playful, and above all enjoying a variety of smells added up to the perfect day in the world of the African wild dog.

From the viewing area a bit further along the boardwalk, guests looked down upon a four-acre savanna-like setting covered with a few shade trees, both tall and short grasses, and high platforms the dogs could use as lookouts. Large boulders created hiding places and caves they used as dens. Coconuts and pinecones carrying a variety of scents along with antlers shed by the reindeer living in the European exhibit were scattered throughout the exhibit for the dogs to chew or play ferocious games of tug of war with. Visitors young and old enjoyed watching the dogs interact with these objects.

Alice changed their playthings quite often with the goal of keeping the dogs stimulated. In her opinion, the most fun occurred the day after Halloween, when local stores donated pumpkins that Alice and her crew stuffed with meat and hid throughout the exhibit. The dogs hunted, rolled, chased, pounced on, guarded, and chewed these pumpkins, entertaining themselves and observers for hours.

Alice's first job of the day was to clean and check the exhibit area. This was a dirty job. She bagged waste, checked for objects such as broken antlers that might injure the dogs, looked for poison ivy growth, washed water troughs, and checked for anything unusual or abnormal that might have made its way in to the exhibit overnight. This was a critical step in caring for the safety of her dogs and was something she did daily. It took about an hour to complete this task.

Feeding the dogs came next. The African wild dog diet isn't like the diet of other dogs. Most dogs are omnivores, eating both meat and plants, but African wild dogs are exclusively carnivores. Alice served the meat raw while the dogs were still in their pens, females in one and males in the other. She fed the dogs each morning and evening, always out of sight of the public, because it was sometimes hard for guests to watch the reality of life as a carnivore.

She procured the meat from two sources. One was a company that raised and butchered animals specifically for zoos. Alice ordered what she needed, and a box arrived at the enclosure twice daily. Depending on the day, it might include chickens, rabbits, goats, beef, or hard-boiled eggs.

Alice's second source of meat was more unconventional and was based upon the relationships she'd established with farmers in the region. When a farmer needed to put an animal down due to old age, illness, or an accident, he'd call Alice, who would send a vet to evaluate the situation. If the animal was put down, it was brought to the zoo, butchered, and fed to the dogs. This provided the farmer with a humane way to end his animal's life and a natural way to dispose of the animal, save money, and sometimes save lives, since the vet occasionally determined that the animal in question didn't need to be put down. It had taken a lot of work to establish this program and to persuade the zoo's directors it would be safe and healthy, but it was unquestionably a success.

As Alice opened the food box, the pens suddenly came alive with high-pitched cries of excitement. She fed the three males first, then the anxiously waiting females, eight in all. Today, she threw three goat carcasses to the boys, while the girls received an assortment of chickens, rabbits, and mice.

The dogs immediately circled the meat and ate with great pleasure. White-tipped tails wagged and satisfied grumbles could be heard. Alice watched her pack with satisfaction, washed her hands, and began sweeping the dog's walkway to the gate leading outside.

When they finished eating, Alice entered the keeper's area from which she could safely release the pack. There, she began the gating procedures that followed each morning meal and brought the dogs back in each night for safekeeping. This was a necessary step, since zoos all over the world had experienced nighttime break-ins in which animals had been harmed.

African wild dogs are intelligent, and it had only taken Alice and Tom, the assistant keeper, days to train the pack. One blow of the whistle told the dogs to line up at the pen's gated door. Next, two whistles and a push of a lever opened the pen's door and the gate leading to the entrance pen. This pen had a door on each side, one leading outside and one inside. Once the inside door closed and the dogs were secure, the outside door opened.

Alice first released the boys, then the girls, into the enclosure. Each dog flew out the door, eager to explore, find a new toy or smell, or just experience the thrill of being first. It was a bit like letting kids out for recess after a long day at school, and the dogs' joy was as obvious as any child's.

CHAPTER TWO

Abandoned

◆ ◆ ◆

SHE WAS WET. She was cold. She was hungry.

It had been two long days since this purebred black lab had been abandoned in an unfamiliar city a hundred miles north of the Foxmoore Area Zoo.

Surrounded by unfamiliar and frightening noises as well as unusual sights and smells, she had taken refuge in an alley behind a dumpster used by a Chinese restaurant, a Greek delicatessen, and several nearby apartments.

The contents of the dumpster were in the process of rotting. Accompanying the putrid odor were thousands of insects. They swarmed the lab's body, finding their way into her nose and ears as well as the milk oozing from the pouches lining her belly. She had delivered

a litter of puppies only a few days earlier, but at birth her pups had been lifeless. The tiny motionless bodies had been removed immediately, despite the lab's frantic efforts to lick life into them. After that, she'd been loaded into a vehicle, driven into the city, and dumped. Though her pups were gone, her milk flowed.

In the early afternoon following a rainy night, the sun finally appeared from behind the clouds. Although she was famished, the dog began to feel better as her fur dried. Unfortunately, the sun also seemed to give the insects more energy. Some of the irritating creatures began burrowing into her body. Confused by all that had happened to her in the past several days, the lab was careful to stay hidden.

When darkness came, the noises and movement around the dumpster increased. People walked and talked in the alley and in the buildings around her, and great bags of garbage were tossed overhead while sirens screeched and loud music blared. She heard rats scratching at the bags that missed the dumpster, seeking their evening meal.

A familiar smell suddenly hit her nose, and she realized it was coming from under the dumpster. It was a bag that contained uneaten meat, and its smell made her stomach growl. She quietly crawled to the end of the dumpster, her nose close to the ground. Once she located the bag, she slid her paw inside, but a hungry rat had already discovered the bag. When the lab spread her toes to grab her meal, the rat savagely bit her tender flesh.

The dog yelped, her own cries frightening her, then froze. She smelled the air to see if she had attracted any unwanted attention. The rat bit her a second time, but now the dog stayed silent. Squeezing her eyes shut, she grasped the meat firmly and pulled.

The rat followed the coveted prize, sticking its noise and whiskers out from the bag, but the dog had reached her limit. She lowered her head and gave a quick sharp bark.

That was enough for the rat. It abandoned the meat for treasures less dangerously acquired and scuttled off.

The dog gulped her food out of fear that some other creature might try to take it. Then she licked her tender bites, curled up, and fell asleep.

At sunrise, a chill still hanging in the air, a fierce noise entered the alley, bouncing off the buildings with a great roar. Tremendous wheels, hissing air brakes, and screeching metal entered her world. The dumpster began to rise from the asphalt, higher and higher, blocking what little sun shone in the sky.

"Hey, hang on a minute," a voice suddenly said. "I see something."

The dumpster stopped moving. A man jumped off the back of the truck and approached her.

"What do we have here? It's a dog. Oh man, she's a mother. We've got to get her outta here and to the shelter. Her puppies must be lookin' for their mama."

The man picked up the frightened but friendly lab and placed her on the front seat of the truck's cab. Again, great sounds came from the truck as it lowered the dumpster back into position. After throwing a few torn bags into the rear of the truck, the man jumped to his place at the back and off it roared.

The truck's cab was warm and ragged and smelled of cigarettes, oil, and garbage.

The environment seemed friendly, but the confused dog did not know what to do. She sat quietly, making a point not to look at the driver. She was afraid she'd be thrown out just like she had been a few days earlier, after her puppies had been taken from her.

After a short drive, the truck pulled up to a worn cement building, its arrival causing a lot of commotion. Dogs began barking, and a murder of crows flew up from the trees behind the shelter.

The door of the cab opened with a tug and a jerk.

"Come on, sweetie. The sooner we get you in here, the sooner your folks can find you. They must be missin' you for sure."

The man from the back of the truck carried her through the door and placed her feet first on the cement floor.

The dog lifted the paw with the rat bites and limped to the desk.

"What have we got here?" a curious voice asked.

"Found her behind a dumpster in Chinatown. She must be missin' her puppies. Full of fleas and lice she is. She's got some nasty breath, too."

"Okay. Come back here, poor girl. We'll see if anyone calls for you."

With that, the garbage man exited the door, never to be seen again.

Henry, the shelter attendant, led the worn dog down a long hallway lined with pens. Each pen had a chain link gate and a cement floor with a drain in the middle. The drain made cleaning up after the inhabitants easy.

"In you go. I'll be back in a bit with your food, water, and information."

The door shut with a bang and was secured with a metal hook. Her food and water were delivered as promised and a card slid into the holder on the gate. It read

"Female, Lactating, Found in Chinatown 3-17, termination 3-21."

"Hope someone is looking for you, girl. If not, you're gonna meet your maker, but I guess we all meet our maker someday. Don't let those fleas bite you too bad."

The lab had found a shelter that provided food, water, warmth, and protection from rats, but it was a "kill shelter." Dogs that weren't claimed in seven days were put to sleep. The lab had earned seven extra days because she was a mother, or so everyone thought.

The sad, patient dog stretched out on the floor and gave a great sigh, the coolness of the cement soothing her aching, milk-engorged breasts. There she waited and waited and waited, though for what, she didn't know. Not only had her puppies been born lifeless, but no one was coming for her, but only she knew that.

CHAPTER THREE

What Is an African Wild Dog?

$\bullet \ \bullet \ \bullet$

WITH THE DOGS RELEASED FOR THE DAY, Alice left the protected area, approached the gate, and gazed over the exhibit. She was so proud of her pack of African wild dogs.

In Latin and Greek, these dogs were known as *Lycaon pictus*, or painted wolf, and the name was appropriate. Alice never grew tired of looking at their short coats smudged with hues of red, black, brown, white, and tan. Amazingly, the artist known as Mother Nature colored no two dogs alike, making it easier to tell them apart.

The dogs looked very noble and simultaneously comical, standing tall on long slender legs, tilting their heads this way and that, their large bat ears twisting and turning. Each dog sported black circles around its eyes, looking as if nature had played a practical joke. Tails capped with white tassels waved with pleasure. Though Alice loved watching them, today she couldn't dawdle. She had pens to clean, records to update, and a presentation to review.

Alice heard the keeper's gate rattle as Tom arrived. He had reported early, knowing she needed extra help while she spoke with the guests. Her upcoming talk — the first of many, she hoped — had been advertised on the local television and radio stations and in the newspaper. Rumor had it that a reporter might even be present. Both Alice and Tom hoped the event would bring much-needed donations their dogs' way.

The zoo had hardly been open half an hour when people began milling around the exhibit. Alice had just enough time to glance through her notes and gather her confidence before it was time to mingle.

Once she reached the front of the exhibit, she finally relaxed. Everyone was excited to see the dogs, playful in the early morning air. By afternoon, they would all be napping in the warm sun or in their burrows and not nearly as exciting to watch.

Alice found the microphone and tapped. Yes, it was on. She took a final calming breath and began.

"Good morning, and welcome to the wild African savanna!"

As Alice spoke, the crowd turned toward her.

"My name is Alice Lee, and I'm a zookeeper here at the Foxmoore Area Zoo, but before we get started, I'd like to ask all the children to come to the front — I want to make sure everyone can see these magnificent African wild dogs."

The crowd rearranged itself, ready to learn, as Alice swept her arm out, encompassing her surroundings.

"As I said a few moments ago, welcome to the savanna. In addition to the Grants zebra, the savanna elephant, and the caracal or desert lynx, the grassy plains of Africa are home to the African wild dog, called *mbwa mwitu* in Swahili." Alice paused a moment to let the unfamiliar words sink in.

"Although these dogs are distant relatives of the dogs you have at home, please make no mistake — they are wild and dangerous. These dogs are also called the wolves of Africa, but African wild dogs and wolves do differ. Because this species is endangered," she explained, "the African wild dog has a place in our zoo. Our job is to learn as much as we can about this magnificent animal, and our goal is to keep it a viable part of the African ecosystem."

With her audience listening intently to every word, Alice continued with her talk.

"African wild dogs, or painted dogs as they're sometimes called, are very social, meaning they take care of one another. They are nomadic, following herds of animals that usually provide their next meal. The males hunt in packs, pursuing everything from zebras to hares. They catch the sick and weak animals, and this is good, because it allows the healthy animals to survive and reproduce.

"As you look at the dogs," Alice gestured toward the enclosure, "you can distinguish the males from the females by size — the male is larger. One male leads the entire pack — he's known as the alpha dog. The alpha dog's mate is the only female to give birth. The entire pack helps raise the puppies and care for the nursing mother. After about five months, the pups join the pack. Most litters are big," she explained, "somewhere between ten and nineteen pups. That's why Mom requires a lot of help!"

"Excuse me?" A young woman in the front of the crowd raised her hand.

"Yes, do you have a question?" Alice asked.

"It may be a silly question, but why do only two dogs mate? Wouldn't it be better for the pack if all the females had pups?"

Alice smiled. "That's a very good question. It's important for the pack's survival that each dog has a different job. Some bear pups, some are caregivers, and others hunt. This way, all the needs of the pack are met. That said," she added, "there have been occasions when a subordinate male and female have mated and had a litter. The couple will be forced to leave the pack and find a new territory to form a pack of their own, but this is very rare."

After talking for almost an hour, Alice concluded with a lengthy question-and-answer session and a reminder that donations could be made to the African wild dog exhibit at the gift shop. "Please play a part in their survival," she implored the crowd, "and don't miss the stuffed animals and fabulous posters also available in the gift shop!"

The zookeeper was exhausted by the time the event ended, but it was extremely gratifying to be able to inform others about the animals she loved so dearly.

CHAPTER FOUR

The Wait

◆ ◆ ◆

AS PATIENT AS SHE WAS, it seemed to the lab that she'd been waiting forever for something to happen.

Unfortunately, the only action involved the fleas and lice that continued to feast on her. She'd scratched some places raw seeking relief, but all she'd done was make herself more uncomfortable. At least she received a kind pat on the head and a few gentle words whenever her keeper filled her bowls with food and water.

"Well girl, things aren't going too well, are they?" Henry shook his head. "I was sure someone would come looking for you. Time is growing short."

The lab put her head back down on her paws, sighed, and tried not to scratch.

CHAPTER FIVE

Highly Unlikely

◆ ◆ ◆

AFTER A LONG BUT PLEASANT DAY, it was finally time to bring the dogs in for the evening. Alice was grateful for Tom's help as the whistle blew and the dogs lined up at the gate.

"What's with Bella?" Tom suddenly asked. "Look," he pointed. "She's dragging her hindquarters on the ground, and the others won't go near her. I've never heard her cry like that before."

Alice looked at Bella with concern. Inexplicably, the young African wild dog wasn't following the gating routine. Instead, she was pacing back and forth and shaking her head as though something were caught in her ear.

"Leave her alone and get the rest of them in," Alice told Tom. "I'll have to go out."

Alice hurriedly put on her bite suit made of suede leather and multiple layers of padding. It covered her from her neck to her boots. Next she secured the helmet and pulled its cage down over her face. The last piece of protective equipment was her gloves, which were protective but amazingly flexible. By the time she was dressed, all the dogs but Bella were in. Clearly, something was up, but what could it be?

As Alice entered the exhibit, Bella sought cover under a nearby bush. Approaching slowly to avoid distressing her further, Alice noticed swelling along Bella's abdomen and discharge from her hindquarters.

Alice felt stunned.

Could Bella have given birth? She was barely an adult and a long way from being the alpha female, but the signs were unmistakable.

Alice thought back to the question the visitor had asked earlier that day. It might be very rare, but a subordinate female did occasionally breed with a subordinate male.

Alice left Bella in the bush and began systematically searching the exhibit. As big as it was, it had to be done.

Some time later, her heart pounding, Alice suddenly heard the tiniest of cries.

The zookeeper looked around frantically until she

spotted a den-like area between two large rocks. It was small, but Bella was small too, and she could have wiggled inside to give birth.

Squatting on the ground, Alice reached inside the den. This could have been dangerous if Bella had wanted to protect her pups, but she was clearly avoiding the area.

Alice touched a small body and carefully pulled a tiny black and white puppy from the den. She reached in again and pulled out another pup. She reached in a third time, but the den was now empty.

Tucking the two pups inside her blouse beneath her bite suit, Alice nestled them against her warm skin, then called to Tom to get on the radio and contact Kate, the vet on duty. This was an emergency.

With the puppies squirming under her shirt, she walked toward Bella, who was still cowering in the bushes. With her tail between her legs and her head down, her eyes squeezed closed, the young dog was clearly behaving like a subordinate female.

Dropping bits of raw meat, Alice was able to coax Bella to follow her in. She guided her to a dog crate where the vet could examine her.

It was a matter of minutes before the vet arrived.

After placing a soft, see-through muzzle on Bella, Kate performed a brief examination.

"Yep. She has indeed given birth," the vet confirmed. "Having only two pups is highly unusual, but this entire situation is unusual."

As baffled as she was that two subordinate African wild dogs had mated, Alice knew she needed to set this mystery aside, at least for the time being, and focus on getting Bella and her pups to the zoo's hospital and into isolation. This was for their own protection — the remainder of the pack would not tolerate the presence of these unexpected intruders.

"Tom, would you close the exhibit?" she asked. "I have a long night ahead of me and a mystery to try to solve."

"There are mysteries in nature every day, Alice. This one is not so mysterious as it is unusual. Just take care of these treasures Bella has brought into the world the best you can."

"Thanks, Tom." Alice gave him a grateful look. "That is exactly what I needed to hear."

Alice and Kate transported the dogs to the zoo's hospital in the hospital van. The pups were chilled and most likely hadn't eaten, as Bella had apparently abandoned them as soon as they were born. They needed immediate attention, as did their confused and disoriented mother, who sat quivering in her carrier.

Kate called ahead and had her attendants prepare a simple pen of recycled cardboard bedding with a heat lamp in a corner. Food stuffed with supplements for nursing canines and a water bowl waited in another corner.

At the hospital, after thoroughly examining Bella and cleaning her up, Kate confirmed that she carried no more pups and was in remarkably good shape. Her milk was even beginning to come in.

Kate then examined the pups. Their low body temperature and lack of nourishment were a concern, but otherwise they appeared to be like any other newborn African wild dog pups.

There was no time to waste. The pups needed to be reunited with their mother and given an opportunity to nurse and bond with her, so Alice and Kate placed Bella in the pen directly under the heat light and set the pups down beside her. She still wore the see-through muzzle, as there was still a strong possibility of her causing harm to her puppies.

Bella tolerated the puppies initially, but when they sought her milk and began nursing, she let out a distressed cry. With her tail between her legs, she ran to the far side of the pen, the pups dangling from her.

As the little bundles fell to the floor, Bella turned to look at them. She cautiously nudged each pup with her nose. Then, her tail between her legs and her eyes bulging with fear, she ran to the corner and turned her back on everyone.

"Bella, please take care of your puppies." Tears rolling down her cheeks, Alice shook her head. "This cannot be happening. She cannot be rejecting these pups."

"It's not supposed to happen," Kate agreed, "but it is happening, and we need to figure it out fast."

Still suited up, Alice unlatched the pen's door, walked in, and knelt down. She cradled one of the puppies in her gloved hands and held it out to Bella.

"Please, Bella," she begged. "Please accept your puppies."

Bella buried her head in the cardboard fluff and dug at the floor. She showed her teeth, squatted, and peed.

Kate shook her head. "She is clearly in distress. We must take the pups from her before she tries to do away with them. She is too young to have participated in a birthing experience with her mother, so she doesn't understand. Come on, Alice. Let me help you out of there before she begins to act like the wild dog she is."

Alice nodded, tears streaming down her face. "She may not accept these pups, but I will not have them bond with humans," she vowed. "They are African wild dogs, and wild they will be."

"I agree, but for now they need to be nourished and kept warm. I'll warm up a couple of bottles of canine breast milk and be right back."

Keeping a careful eye on Bella, Alice took both puppies and set them in a nest of towels on the examination table. She placed a folding chair next to the table and attached a second heat lap to the table's edge. She quickly removed her bite suit and helmet, but keeping her gloves on, she gathered additional towels and a container of sanitary wipes.

These dogs were not going to bond with her if she could help it, but there was no way she could avoid giving them their first nourishment and warmth. The pups' eyes were closed, so sight wouldn't be a problem. It was scent she had to worry about. How was she going to make herself smell like an African wild dog?

Alice spotted the answer lying at the other end of the examination table.

She gathered the soiled towels Kate had used to clean Bella and began rubbing them over her own clothing.

Who cared if this were unpleasant? All that mattered was that she would smell like the pups' mother.

By the time Kate returned, Alice was seated next to the examination table under the heat lamp, the pups cradled in her arms.

She took the warm bottles of milk from Kate and slid them into the puppies' small black mouths. When they immediately began sucking, Alice felt encouraged. This was a good sign.

While the dogs were nursing, Kate prepared their bed. She placed a heating pad in the bottom half of a dog crate and covered it with a wool blanket and a few towels that held their mother's scent. She then carefully hung the heat lamp from a corner. Warmth was incredibly important. Without it, the pups would quickly die.

When the bed was ready and the bottles were empty, Alice moved the pups to the crate, careful to maintain their physical contact with one another. Now that they had warm full tummies, they were sleepy. By the time she set them down and latched the door to the crate, they were sound asleep.

"I think I have a plan," Alice told Kate, gazing at the tiny pups. "First I'm going to get on the computer and contact the African Wild Dog Association and see if I can find a zoo with a lactating female that could foster these guys. It's probably not a possibility, given how early in the year they've been born, but it's worth a try."

"What if you can't find a lactating African wild dog?" Kate asked.

"I'll have to look for a lactating domestic animal," Alice replied, pulling off her gloves. "That will at least extend the time we have to look or wait for a wild one."

Kate nodded. "I'll watch the pups tonight," she offered. "They'll need to be fed and their body temperature checked every couple of hours. After you get your computer work done, get some sleep so you can function tomorrow. I'll also call Tom; he can care for the exhibit until you return. Oh, and Dave will be in tomorrow to relieve me." She held a clean lab coat out to Alice. "Put this on and give me your blouse. We'll need to use it when feeding the pups to keep the scent consistent."

Alice unbuttoned her blouse and handed it to Kate. "Dave is going to look great in this," she smiled, struggling into the lab coat Kate handed her in return.

Kate smiled back and draped Alice's blouse over the chair.

Before she left, Alice looked in on Bella. The exhausted dog was sound asleep under her own heat lamp. How confused she must be, poor soul. Bella would sleep at the hospital one night and be returned to

the African wild dog exhibit tomorrow, where she would
hopefully be accepted by her pack without difficulty.

CHAPTER SIX

RED TAG DAY

◆ ◆ ◆

"OH MAN, RED TAG DAY," Henry said gloomily as he placed a small red disc on the dog's gate. The vivid color warned visitors that this was the final day this dog could be adopted before it would be put down.

"I don't understand why people are so mean." He spoke sympathetically to the lab. "I know you're a good dog. The problem is, we've only got a day to make things right for you. I hope we can do it."

Shaking his head, the attendant walked back down the dimly lit hall. At his desk, he turned on the easy listening radio station he enjoyed and glanced at his paperwork. He'd had an easy morning, but he hated putting that red tag on the gate. He'd already made arrangements for the vet to come put the dog down the next morning, assuming she was still there, and it sure looked like she would be.

This was the hard part of his job; he knew he'd never get used to it.

Don't think about it. Don't think about it.

Henry signed, pulled himself closer to his desk, and hummed to the music on the radio.

CHAPTER SEVEN

Day Two with Bella's Pups

◆ ◆ ◆

ALICE WOKE EARLY, her entire body stiff, her mind immediately jumping to yesterday's events.

Wincing, she stumbled out of bed and to her computer, but it was just as she'd thought — no one had responded positively to her inquiry. It was simply too early in the year for lactating African wild dogs.

She found a dog at a zoo about a thousand miles away due to give birth in three weeks, but that did Bella's pups no good; they needed a foster mother right away.

As soon as she was dressed, Alice headed to the hospital to check on the pups. She held back an involuntary giggle when she saw Dave, Kate's veterinarian colleague, wrapped up in her blouse, feeding his charges.

"You look gorgeous, Dave!"

"Don't I, though? I'm a regular wild dog!"

Alice took a closer look at the pups. They appeared to be doing well, but she wouldn't be happy until they were being nursed by a canine, and it was her job to locate one as soon as possible.

Returning to her workstation, Alice located the zoo's list of animal rescue groups and public agencies. She spent the better part of three hours making calls with no luck. She couldn't find a single nursing canine in the area.

Alice paced, brooding, and then she had an idea.

Taking the cell phone from her pocket, she studied the contacts list. There it was, the radio station that had promoted her lecture. Surely they would put out a bulletin for a foster canine mother.

Alice called and explained the situation. Fewer than ten minutes later, she heard the announcement explaining the zoo's predicament.

"Oh please," she whispered. "This is our last hope. Please, oh please."

CHAPTER EIGHT

Hear Ye, Hear Ye

• • •

HENRY BRIEFLY LEFT THE SHELTER TO PICK UP LUNCH, returning with a vegetable sub for himself and a double quarter pounder for her. If this were going to be her last day on Earth, she was going to have the juicy burger he wished he could eat.

As he entered the building, the radio still on, he dropped his lunch on his desk and walked down the hall to give his girl, as he'd begun thinking of her, her treat. He was tempted to take a bite, only one bite, but no — this was her burger.

As Henry began digging into the bag, he heard the music stop and an announcer come over the radio.

That was odd. The station was usually all music

except for the five minutes each hour when the weather came on.

Henry carefully unwrapped the burger so as not to lose any of the juices.

When the lab smelled the aroma, she got up, her tail wagging.

"I know you like that smell, girl. I wish I could share one with you, but the old heart's been acting up, so no salt or fat for me."

Henry slid the burger into the pen and watched her devour it.

"Love you, girl. Now for my lunch. Not as good as yours, but it will do."

Slowly, he made his way back to his desk. There were still a couple more hours of work to be done, and then he was heading home.

Again the music stopped, and the announcer's voice came on.

"Please, the Foxmoore Area Zoo needs your help. They desperately need to locate a lactating canine to foster one of their animals. If you know of any such animal, please call Alice at the zoo or call this station. They'll be very grateful for your help."

What? A lactating canine? He had a lactating canine. What was that number?

Henry reached for his cell phone. He didn't pray often, but he offered a silent prayer now that this was the break his girl so desperately needed.

CHAPTER NINE

On the Fly

● ● ●

ALICE SAT CROSS-LEGGED on the computer chair, a box of dry cereal on her lap. Picking at it, staring at the cell phone on her desk, she willed the phone to ring.

When it did, she jumped, sending cereal flying all over the floor.

She had already received two prank calls; this one had to be real. Praying silently, she answered, "Hello, this is Alice Lee, zookeeper at the Foxmoore Area Zoo. How may I help you?"

"Miss, I think I have a dog for you."

"*Yes!*" she whispered, her fist pumping the air. She cautioned herself not to get too excited. "Tell me about her. Where is she? What's her condition?"

"She's in the Gaylesville Animal Shelter, about a

hundred miles north of where you are. She's been here almost two weeks, but her milk is still flowing. She's got fleas and lice but should clean up all right. She's a good girl. She's going to be put down tomorrow morning if no one calls for her."

"Well, she's the only lactating canine I know of right now. I'll jump in the van and be there as soon as I can." While Alice spoke, she began collecting her things, spilled cereal crunching beneath her feet.

"We close at six. Drive safely."

Alice entered the address of the animal shelter into her phone, yelling to Dave over her shoulder as she left the building, "Taking the van. Got a dog in Gaylesville!"

Opening the back of the van, Alice cleared everything out of the travel cages. She couldn't allow this dog to infest the cargo blankets and rags with fleas and lice. She then jumped into the driver's seat, the engine's roar echoing through the empty cabin.

"Drat. It needs gas."

Fortunately, there was a gas station at the entrance to the highway. Alice stopped, filled the tank, and grabbed a sandwich and a bottle of water. It was a straight hour-and-a-half drive to the shelter, but the trip felt like it took forever.

A million thoughts ran through her mind. She'd need

special shampoo and cleaner to de-flea and delouse the nursing mother. More importantly, would the dog be aggressive or cooperative? Would she accept the abandoned pups or reject them as their own mother had done?

Both hopeful and concerned, Alice headed north.

CHAPTER TEN

Departure

◆ ◆ ◆

HENRY LOOKED AT THE CLOCK. It was a little past five. He hoped that zookeeper would get here soon. He really couldn't take this kind of suspense much longer. If he had to, he'd stay past six. Anything for his girl.

He was pacing back and forth when he heard the van pull into the gravel driveway. Hurrying to the door, he peered out. "You the lady from the zoo?"

"I sure am. May I see your dog right away?" Alice went straight to the point. "I have a couple of African wild dog pups desperate for a foster mother."

They walked through the lobby and down the hall, and when they stopped at the lab's pen, Alice caught her breath. There she was, just lying there, waiting for life to happen.

"May I go in?" she asked.

Henry unlatched the gate and opened the door, and Alice approached slowly.

"No need to be worried," Henry said. "She's a nice dog, a very nice girl."

Alice let out a sign of relief as the dog rose to her feet, wagging her tail. She noticed numerous sores from digging at fleas. She also noticed the dog's belly still carried sacks filled with milk.

"You poor girl; you are a mess. I'll take you back and clean you up, and then you have a job to do."

Alice placed the lead she had brought with her around the dog's neck and led her to the lobby.

Henry patted his girl one last time. "We'll need $50.00 for keeping her here." His tone was a bit apologetic.

Alice pulled the money from her pocket, thanked Henry profusely, and made her way to the van. Henry watched with a big grin as the dog obediently jumped into one of the cargo cages and was secured.

"You have a chance at life now, girl," he whispered. "I just hope it's a good one."

CHAPTER ELEVEN

The Blessing

◆ ◆ ◆

THE TRIP HOME WENT A BIT FASTER than the trip north, but not by much. It was a quiet ride, and the dog didn't make a sound. She seemed very placid and accepting.

Both Dave and Kate were waiting when Alice pulled in. She parked, jumped out, and practically ran to the back of the van.

"I think she'll do, but she needs cleaning up fast." Opening the doors, Alice unlatched the travel cage and helped the dog down.

"She looks like my Aunt Lucy's dog Fiona," Kate remarked.

Alice glanced down. The lab was wagging her tail and looking at her expectantly.

Alice smiled. "Well then, Fiona, let's get to work on you."

It took all three of them to get Fiona ready for the pups. They gave her a warm medicated bath, but her first tub of water was so brown and filled with dead or dying fleas and lice that they drew another to make sure she was really clean. Once the bath was complete, they brushed her teeth and examined her sores.

Fiona relished every morsel of attention. She didn't even object to having her teeth cleaned. It had been a long time since she'd had any kind of loving care, and it felt heavenly to be warm, clean, and insect free. After eating a hearty meal filled with vitamins and medications to increase her milk production and improve her health, Fiona felt ready for whatever was about to happen.

As Kate readied a pen for the prospective new family, Alice silently prayed that all would go well. The pups needed a mother, and hopefully, Fiona yearned to be one.

"Ready, girl?" Alice gave Fiona an encouraging look. "Here we go."

She led Fiona into the pen and patted the floor. The dog lay down under the heat lamp as if she knew exactly what she was supposed to do.

When Kate placed the pups in front of her, Fiona

leaned forward and promptly began sniffing. She then began to lick the puppies with her long warm pink tongue.

After a few moments, Alice leaned over and placed each squirming pup near Fiona's abdomen. The pups immediately nuzzled into her fur, found her milk, and began nursing. Fiona closed her eyes, stretched out, and relaxed, the picture of contentment.

Tears streaming down her cheeks, Alice looked over at Kate and Dave, who were also wiping away tears. "How easy was that?" she marveled. It was as if Fiona had been born to be a mother to these pups.

As the days went by, the black lab continued to nurse and care for the two abandoned puppies with great joy. She kept them clean, pulled them close to her when they wiggled off, and slept with them between meals in a pile of three.

Daily, the pups grew stronger and more active. Their eyes opened, their color began to change, and they began to look more and more like the African wild dogs they were.

Fiona was a very happy and successful foster mother, and her adopted African wild dog pups were thriving.

She was the blessing Alice had been looking for.

CHAPTER TWELVE

The Rest of the Story

◆ ◆ ◆

SEVERAL WEEKS AFTER THE LAB left the animal shelter, thoughts of her continued to cross Henry's mind. He considered calling the zoo and checking on her, but he decided not to. If the news was bad, he didn't think he could take it.

Other dogs had come and gone, but this girl had touched his heart.

Henry sighed, switched on the radio, and dug into a mound of paperwork. Suddenly, his music was interrupted and the announcer's voice came on.

"And now the rest of the story, folks. A few weeks back, we sent out a bulletin from Foxmoore Area Zoo looking for a nursing dog. Well, one was found. Her name is Fiona, and she is now the foster mom to two African wild dog pups abandoned by their mother."

The announcement included additional details, but Henry didn't hear them.

"Fiona," he said, testing the name, a grin on his face. "That's a fine name for a fine girl."

CHAPTER THIRTEEN

Wild Should Stay Wild

* * *

AS MUCH AS ALICE LOVED WATCHING the happy little family she had helped create, she knew that if these puppies were going to become real African wild dogs, they had to be raised in an African wild dog pack.

In the pack, the puppies would nurse for five months, all the while developing relationships with other pack members and learning essential skills. Although Fiona was a wonderful mother, Alice had to get the puppies into a pack with a nursing African wild dog mother as soon as possible.

She'd been keeping in touch with the zoo she'd contacted the night the pups were born, the one that had a pregnant African wild dog. After studying the genealogical charts she kept as part of her Species Survival Plan,

Alice felt confident the packs weren't closely related. With that potential issue resolved, the two zoos agreed to try to integrate the abandoned pups with the African wild dog mother after she delivered.

There would be about a four-week age difference between the two sets of puppies, but that wouldn't necessarily be a problem. This mother had already given birth to four healthy litters, so everything hinged on whether or not she decided to accept these pups.

It made Alice sad to think of separating Fiona from her foster litter, but if at all possible, these pups needed to be raised by their own kind. This was the only way they'd become African wild dogs rather than pets.

As Alice waited to hear the news that the African wild dog mother had delivered, she and Kate made plans for the long trip to the Foot Hills Zoo.

CHAPTER FOURTEEN

On Their Way

◆ ◆ ◆

FINALLY, THE FOOT HILLS ZOO CALLED. Their African wild dog mother had delivered a healthy litter, and they were willing and excited to take Fiona's puppies. What's more, they wanted them as soon as possible.

Alice and Kate plotted the thousand-mile trip and decided to break it into two days. They would take turns driving and sleep in the van as needed. Above all, they would create as little stress as possible for their precious cargo.

After filling the van with supplies for people and canines and preparing a special crate, Fiona and her charges were loaded.

Fiona didn't seem to mind all the fuss as long as her

puppies, fat and healthy and increasingly frisky, were by her side.

Dave and Tom said their goodbyes and wished them a safe trip, and soon the van and its special occupants were on their way.

CHAPTER FIFTEEN

The Plan

◆ ◆ ◆

THE KEEPERS AT BOTH THE FOOT HILLS ZOO and the Foxmoore Area Zoo worked hard to develop a plan of introduction and acceptance.

The first phase of the plan was to introduce the new pack to the scent of Fiona and the pups. Accordingly, several of Fiona's blankets were sent to the Foot Hills Zoo, torn into strips, and sprinkled with the African wild dog mother's urine. The blanket pieces were then spread throughout the enclosure for the wild dogs to inspect. The hope was that familiarity with Fiona's and the new pups' scent in association with their dominant female would help the pack accept the new pups.

Meanwhile, a kerchief carrying the African wild dog mother's scent was tied around Fiona's neck for several days to help the pups associate the scent of their new mother with their foster mother.

In phase two, all the dogs would be gated except for the new mother and her newborn pups, who would be in their den in the enclosure. The keepers would dress in their bite suits and helmets and place the two new pups within reach of the mother. If the mother accepted these pups, the rest of the pack would likely do so as well.

The keepers' main concern was the dominant male. If his mate accepted the puppies, he probably would too, assuming he was interested in his mate's approval. If he wasn't, the experiment could end tragically.

Once the mother showed signs of acceptance, the final phase of the plan would be put into motion — releasing the rest of the pack to investigate. First, the females would be released, then the males. The keepers would stay close to the gate should things get violent and they needed to try to recapture the pups.

Of course, everyone knew the odds of rescuing the pups would be slight if a problem occurred. African wild dogs are by nature extremely protective of one another. In addition, they're savage butchers when chasing prey, which they might consider the pups to be, especially if their new mother rejected them.

Only time would tell.

CHAPTER SIXTEEN

Arrival

• • •

THE JOURNEY WASN'T AS DIFFICULT as Alice and Kate had anticipated, and their adrenaline helped keep them awake as the miles slipped by.

The sun was just setting on day two of their journey when they pulled into the rear entrance of the Foot Hills Zoo.

Once the human introductions were made, Alice presented Fiona and her pups to Jordan, the African wild dog keeper at the Foot Hills Zoo. Together, they decided to keep Fiona with her pups one more night and to introduce the pups to their new mother at dawn.

Needless to say, it was going to be a long night.

CHAPTER SEVENTEEN

The Long Night

* * *

AS ANTICIPATED, SLEEP DID NOT come easily. Most of Alice and Kate's time was spent watching Fiona with the pups she loved and mentally rehearsing their plan of action.

Early the next morning, when Jordan knocked on the door, a wakeful Alice dressed in her protective clothing, her hands clumsy with a combination of excitement and anxiety.

It was going to be emotionally difficult to separate Fiona from the pups she loved so much, but Alice simply had no choice.

With Kate and Jordan by her side, murmuring consolations, Alice reached gloved hands into Fiona's crate to avoid transferring her human scent to the pups.

One at a time, she removed the pups from their resting place next to their foster mother and placed them in
a smaller travel crate.

Fiona immediately began to whimper, and Kate got
in her crate with her, stroked her head, and sat beside
her as the door closed. She would stay and comfort Fiona
during the transfer while Alice and Jordan introduced
the pups to their new mother.

CHAPTER EIGHTEEN

To Be or Not to Be?

• • •

HOLDING THE PUPS CLOSE TO HER CHEST, Alice gazed at the African wild dog mother and her pups nestled in a small den at the back of the enclosure.

Nearby, other keepers stood suited and waiting, and Alice knew it was now or never.

"Let's get this show on the road." Though she sounded brave, Alice's uncertainty showed in her eyes.

Jordan placed his hand on her shoulder and smiled, and Alice felt a bit comforted.

Smiling back, she handed him a wiggling puppy.

When the door to the enclosure opened, six keepers began walking toward the den in a "V" formation with Alice and Jordan protected at the point.

They walked within three feet of the alpha female

without stirring much interest and then stopped to avoid angering her.

Jordan and a somewhat reluctant Alice lowered their pups to the still chilly ground and then slowly backed away, making as little noise as possible. Once they'd taken about fifteen giant steps backward, they stopped and stood very still.

It wasn't long before the female raised her nose and captured the scent of the pups, her ears twitching at their cries for their mom.

She stood and stretched as if she hadn't a care in the world, all the while surveying her surroundings. Slowly, she took a step out of the den and then another step toward the pups.

The six keepers held their breath.

One more step, and the female was on top of the pups.

She lowered her head and smelled each pup. Then it happened — she took a pup in her mouth.

This was the moment of truth. Would she accept the puppy, or would she savage it and toss it to the side?

The mother turned and trotted to her den. They watched her deposit the pup next to her own litter of squirming pups. She returned for the next pup, took it in her mouth, and again trotted back to her den. She set the pup down with the others, examined the entire litter, lay down, and began nursing.

The keepers could barely contain themselves. They backed up without turning around, exited the enclosure, and walked silently back to the office.

After closing the door, high fives and cheers erupted. Phase two appeared to be a success, but they would observe the pups and their new mom for several hours before releasing the rest of the females.

Watching the new family through the observation window of the office, Alice was so filled with emotion that she found it difficult to speak.

"Cup of tea?" Jordan offered her a cup and stood with her to watch.

She nodded gratefully. "I'd love one."

After taking a sip of the hot bracing liquid, Alice glanced at Jordan. "As the primary caretaker of this new family, how would you feel about collaborating with me on a paper for the *Zoological Science Journal* about this experience?"

He grinned. "There's nothing I'd like more."

A few hours later, after the African wild dog mother had nursed and cleaned all the pups and the new family had taken a nap, it was time to introduce the females of the pack.

When the whistle blew, the anxious females lined up. They weren't used to being in their pens with the sun so high in the sky, and besides that, they'd caught the scent of new humans and animals. What could be happening?

One by one, Jordan released the subordinate females into the enclosure. Each made a beeline to the pup-filled den and circled the enlarged family, white-tipped tail wagging in the air. After a great deal of sniffing and many high-pitched whining sounds, one by one, each female lost interest, left the den, and began her daily exploration of the enclosure. As the last dog passed in front of the mother, the keepers again concluded that all was well.

The plan seemed to be working, but the male dogs still needed to be released.

Jordan blew the whistle and began releasing the males into the enclosure. Like the females, they headed straight for the den, the alpha dog leading the way.

He inspected the scent trail, the remaining males waiting some distance behind him, and stopped just before the entrance of the den as if making a decision.

Suddenly, his upper lip curled, showing his fierce white teeth. All at once, a savage growl erupted from his quivering throat.

The keepers gasped. What should they do?

"Be patient," whispered Jordan. "This is the show-down we expected. We have to wait it out."

Once again, Jordan rested his hand on Alice's shoulder. She stood frozen, not a muscle moving.

The female stuck her head out of the den, protecting her pups with her body. She went nose to nose with the alpha male, her eyes almost bulging out of their sockets.

Silence.

Suddenly, a flash of teeth and a bigger-than-life bark from the female.

The male stood his ground.

The female emitted a low-pitched growl, then lunged and bit him on the nose.

Still he stood his ground.

The staring and growling seemed to last forever, but finally the male began backing away. After a few moments, he squatted and urinated, marking this family as his, and then walked off, allowing the remaining males a chance to inspect his new family.

This event took far less time, as there wasn't much interest now that the alpha male had reluctantly accepted the pups.

The keepers let out a collective sigh of relief.

"Wow. It seems to have ended well, but I'm not sure

my heart could take another experience like that." Alice's entire body trembled.

Jordan nodded. "I think we're good, but let's stay put a while."

The other keepers melted away, but Alice and Jordan continued observing for several more hours. Late in the afternoon, when the alpha male approached his mate again, he first gave and then received several affectionate face licks.

Alice's heartfelt sigh of relief reflected her supreme satisfaction. It looked like the two orphaned African wild dog pups would be raised by their own kind after all.

CHAPTER NINETEEN

A Job Well Done

• • •

THAT EVENING, AFTER ALL the African wild dogs had been gated and penned except for the new mother and her pups, Alice returned to Kate and Fiona.

A sense of sadness permeated the van, but Fiona's tail thumped when she saw Alice, her nose checking for her pups.

"It's okay, girl," Alice told her, crawling into her crate with her. "Your babies have a new mom who will love and raise them well. You should be very proud of the job you did. I know I'm proud of you."

Alice sat down next to Fiona, leaned back against the side of the crate, and immediately fell sound asleep.

Fiona sighed, placed her head on Alice's knee, and dozed off.

Early the next morning, Alice, Kate, and Fiona headed for home, their mission complete. The pups were now Jordan's charges and would be well cared for. Alice had her own pack of African wild dogs to get back to, and Kate had an entire zoo to care for.

CHAPTER TWENTY

The Ride Home

· · ·

THE RIDE HOME WAS UNEVENTFUL. The first day, Alice and Kate were almost completely silent. The separation had been emotionally difficult for humans and canine alike, and everyone was exhausted.

The second day, talk of the zoo and their responsibilities resumed. Kate checked her e-mail during the return trip and confirmed that Alice's pack was doing well. According to Dave and Tom, they'd accepted Bella with little fuss. Bella in turn seemed happy and was once again forming a close bond with her mother.

Something else had happened, too. A young male cheetah had been placed at a zoo out west as part of its cheetah Species Survival Plan. It was hoped he would become a father in a year or so. The problem was, his sister had been left behind. She was very depressed, barely eating, and would not leave the spot where she'd last seen her brother. She appeared to be waiting for his return.

"She'll work though it," Alice said sympathetically. "They always seem to."

"Maybe," Kate replied, "but sometimes I worry about what we're doing. I know in my heart it's right to save these endangered species; I just wish we didn't need to do it from behind walls."

"I know," Alice sighed. "There's so much we humans have to learn. For starters, we have to stop taking habitat that doesn't belong to us. The animals could then reproduce and live healthy lives where they belong."

"Speaking of belonging," Kate asked, "I'm wondering what your plans are for Fiona. Her job is done. Have you thought about what's to become of her?"

"No, I haven't," Alice replied, a worried expression on her face. "Quite frankly, that's another problem that needs a solution."

CHAPTER TWENTY-ONE

A Purpose for Fiona

♦♦♦

WHEN THE VAN PULLED ONTO THE ZOO GROUNDS late that afternoon, all three ladies were glad to get out and stretch their legs.

Alice took Fiona with her to her office, anxious to catch up on mail and recent news. The lab was compliant but subdued, and after several hours, as the sun began to set, Alice decided a walk was in order.

"Fiona, want to walk with me?"

The lab's thumping tail said she'd definitely welcome the distraction.

Out the door and off to the Asian exhibit they went, Alice following Fiona as she walked and sniffed. Several visitors stopped to pet her, and they seemed to enjoy her as much as they did the exotic Middle Eastern animals surrounding them.

As Alice and Fiona continued to stroll, the air lost some of its heat and a cool breeze blew across the exhibit's pond. Alice felt a comfortable calmness come over her.

Fiona, on the other hand, did not seem calm. Her gate quickened into a trot as she headed toward the cheetah exhibit.

Alice remembered the lonely female Kate had mentioned and quickened her step to keep up.

When she turned the corner, she saw Fiona standing next to the young cheetah's enclosure. The dog was trying to reach her paw through the double fence to touch the cheetah's back. Meanwhile, her tongue was going a mile a minute, trying to reach the cat's face.

Slowly, the cheetah turned and allowed her face to be licked.

Alice could hear the cat's rumbling purr begin from where she was standing.

Still licking, Fiona flopped down onto the grass next to the enclosure's fence. In a moment, the cheetah was resting beside her, purring and closing her eyes in bliss.

Alice hurried toward the lab. "Fiona, you are a

miracle worker! You are a great mother *and* a wonderful companion."

The zookeeper's eyes suddenly widened. "I know what we'll do with you!" she said excitedly. "We'll make you a zoo dog! You can roam the grounds and greet visitors. You can also keep our lonely or sad animals company. Just please don't lick the spots off that cheetah!" she added.

Fiona's tail thumped as she returned to the task at hand, comforting the lonesome young cheetah.

Alice left her there and walked back toward her office, reflecting on this most amazing and empathetic of dogs and the immense contribution she'd only just begun to make.

Fiona had found her purpose in life: to offer love and comfort to those in need.

What greater purpose could any soul have?

EPILOGUE

◆ ◆ ◆

IN 1854 DURING TREATY NEGOTIATIONS Chief Seattle spoke these words:

"Teach your children what we have taught our children: that the earth is our mother. Whatever befalls the earth, befalls the children of the earth. If we spit upon the ground we spit upon ourselves. This we know. The earth does not belong to us; we belong to the earth. One thing we know which the white man may one (day) discover, our God is the same God. You may think now that you own him as you wish to own our land; but you cannot. He is the God of all people. And compassion is equal for all. This earth is precious to God, and to harm the earth is to heap contempt on the creator. So love it as we have loved it. Care for it as we have cared for it. With all your mind, with all your heart, pre-serve it for our children and love as God loves us all." — Chief Seattle (goodreads.com)

The Earth, its flora and its fauna must be protected, must grow strong, and must keep the world healthy for our children.

Fiona Finds Her Purpose is based on an actual event. Animal cruelty, species extinctions, and environmental ignorance continue today. On a positive note, there are people willing to step out and intervene on the behalf of the Earth and its flora and fauna.

Be one of those people!

Move into a career of conservation, support conservation efforts through donations of time and or money. Be cognizant each day of the living world around you and to the best of your ability treat it with respect. Educate others by thought, word and deed.

Photographs courtesy of: @windows2thewild.

While hiking on a savannah in South Africa a @windows2thewild photographer had the good fortune to meet up with a pack of African Wild Dogs. He was able to observe and capture images of these magnificent predators in their natural habitat. Thank you for sharing this rare experience.

KAREN RIESER

About the Author

A storyteller by nature, Karen Rieser threads together both fact and fiction to deliver her message. Her love of nature, her desire for all animals to be treated ethically, and a yearning to know the rest of the story motivated her to write, *Fiona Finds Her Purpose*.

Karen's career as an educator and mother of twins was spent in Portage, MI. As an empty-nester, she continued teaching and studied to be a docent at a nearby zoo. It was here she heard the story of a very parasite-infested dog that had been found just in time to foster a pair of abandoned African Wild dog puppies. Using only that information, Karen researched and created *Fiona Finds Her Purpose*.

Karen moved to Traverse City, MI, upon retirement, and now spends her time substitute teaching, traveling, freelance writing, and enjoying artistic endeavors.

The messages taught in Fiona's story are important: respect life regardless of its form, the understanding that the Earth must be cared for, and that we all play a part in one another's survival.